For Tess, you light my world … – S. M.

For all those who love and care for our beautiful world – C. S.

tiger tales
5 River Road, Suite 128, Wilton, CT 06897
Published in the United States 2018
Originally published in Great Britain 2018
by Little Tiger Press
Text copyright © 2018 Stacey McCleary
Illustrations copyright © 2018 Carmen Saldaña / Good Illustration Ltd
ISBN-13: 978-1-68010-082-2
ISBN-10: 1-68010-082-3
Printed in China
LTP/1800/2241/0118

For more insight and activities,
visit us at www.tigertalesbooks.com

I Give You the World

by Stacey McCleary

Illustrated by
Carmen Saldaña

tiger tales

When you were born, so precious and new,
I searched high and low for a gift just for you.

I searched through the day,
and I searched through the night …

...'til I came across this one—
I think it's just right ....

I give you the world and everything in it.
Come, let me show you—
it will take just a minute . . . .

I give to you the dawn's sweet dew,
the morning light just peeking through.

I give to you the spring's soft breeze
that whispers to the tiny seeds.

I give to you the croaking frogs,
the muddy pigs, the sleeping dogs.

I give to you the buzzing bees,
the baby birds—in nests, in trees.

The dolphins dancing just for you,
the whales that sing through oceans blue.

I give to you the sun's warm glow,
the summer rain ...

...the rainbow!

The clouds through which
great mountains rise,

the eagles soaring
through the skies.

I give to you the falling leaves,
floating down upon the breeze.

The animals, both young and old,
preparing for the winter cold.

I give to you the timid doe,
    stepping through fresh fallen snow.

I give to you the day that's done,
    the fading light, the sinking sun.

The hooting owl, the pale moonlight,
the stars that sparkle
through the night.

My gift is each and every thing:
each autumn day, and each new spring,

The winter's chill, the summer's laughter,
every season ever after . . . .

The wonder, the beauty, the magic unfurled . . .
all this is for you . . .

I give you the world.